MW00907267

STORIES OF ROBIN HOOD

Then, still bareheaded, he stood up and swore an oath.

STORIES OF

ROBIN HOOD

TOLD TO THE CHILDREN BY

H. E. MARSHALL

WITH PICTURES BY

A. S. FORREST

YESTERDAY'S CLASSICS

CHAPEL HILL, NORTH CAROLINA

Cover and arrangement © 2005 Yesterday's Classics.

This edition, first published in 2005 by Yesterday's Classics, is an unabridged republication of the work originally published by T. C. & E. C. Jack in 1907. The color illustrations by A. S. Forrest in that volume are rendered in black and white in this edition. For a complete listing of the books published by Yesterday's Classics, please visit www.yesterdaysclassics.com. Yesterday's Classics is the publishing arm of the Baldwin Project which presents the complete text of dozens of classic books for children at www.mainlesson.com under the editorship of Lisa M. Ripperton and T. A. Roth.

ISBN-10: 1-59915-001-8

ISBN-13: 978-1-59915-001-7

Yesterday's Classics
PO Box 3418
Chapel Hill, NC 27515

TO

GRAHAM AND ROBIN

Dear Jos,—Robin Hood was a real man. The stories about him are very old. They were written many, many years ago by men whose names have been forgotten. The old letters in which they were printed are very difficult to read, but now, in this little book, you will find the stories easy both to read and to understand. The poetry is in the same words as it was in those old books.

Robin Hood lived in times very different from ours. In the first chapter of this book I have told you about those times, and how and why Robin came to live in the Green Wood, and to have all his wonderful adventures.

If you do not care about the "how and why," you must begin the book at its second chapter, but I hope you will begin at the beginning, for the more you know about brave Robin, the more you will love and admire him.—Your loving Aunt,

H.E. MARSHALL

CONTENTS

I

HOW ROBIN HOOD CAME TO LIVE IN THE GREEN WOOD

Very many years ago there ruled over England a king, who was called Richard Cœur de Lion. Cœur de Lion is French and means lion-hearted. It seems strange that an English king should have a French name. But more than a hundred years before this king reigned, a French duke named William came to England, defeated the English in a great battle, and declared himself king of all that southern part of Britain called England.

He brought with him a great many Frenchmen, or Normans, as they were called from the name of the part of France over which this duke ruled. These Normans were all poor though they were very proud and haughty. They came with Duke William to help him fight because he promised to give them money and lands as a reward. Now Duke William had not a great deal of money nor many lands of his own. So when he had beaten the English, or Saxons, as they were called in those days, he stole lands and houses, money and cattle from the Saxon nobles and gave them to the Normans. The

Saxon nobles themselves had very often become the servants of these proud Normans. Thus it came about that two races lived in England, each speaking their own language, and each hating the other.

This state of things lasted for a very long time. Even when Richard became king, more than a hundred years after the coming of Duke William, there was still a great deal of hatred between the two races.

Richard Cœur de Lion, as his name tells you, was a brave and noble man. He loved danger; he loved brave men and noble deeds. He hated all mean and cruel acts, and the cowards who did them. He was ever ready to help the weak against the strong, and had he stayed in England after he became king he might have done much good. He might have taught the proud Norman nobles that true nobility rests in being kind and gentle to those less strong and less fortunate than ourselves, and not in fierceness and cruelty.

Yet Richard himself was neither meek nor gentle. He was indeed very fierce and terrible in battle. He loved to fight with people who were stronger or better armed than himself. He would have been ashamed to hurt the weak and feeble.

But Richard did not stay in England. Far, far over the seas there is a country called Palestine. There our Lord was born, lived, and died. Christian people in all ages must think tenderly and gratefully of that far-off country. But at this time it had fallen into the hands of the heathen. It seemed to Christian people in those days that it would be a terrible sin to allow wicked heathen to live in the Holy Land. So they gathered together great armies of brave men from every country in the world and sent them to try to win it back. Many brave deeds were done, many terrible battles fought, but still the heathen kept possession.

Then brave King Richard of England said he too would fight for the city of our Lord. So he gathered together as much money as he could find, and as many brave men as would follow him, and set out for the Holy Land. Before he went away he called two bishops who he thought were good and wise men, and said to them: "Take care of England while I am gone. Rule my people wisely and well, and I will reward you when I return." The bishops promised to do as he asked. Then he said farewell and sailed away.

Now King Richard had a brother who was called Prince John. Prince John was quite different from King Richard in every way. He was not at all a nice man. He was jealous of Richard because he was king, and angry because he himself had not been chosen to rule while Richard was in Palestine. As soon as his brother had gone, John went to the bishops and said, "You must let me rule while the king is away." And the bishops allowed him to do so. Deep down in his wicked heart John meant to make himself king altogether, and never let Richard come back any more.

A sad time now began for the Saxons. John tried to please the haughty Normans because they were great and powerful, and he hoped they would help to make him king. He thought the best way to please them was to give them land and money. So as he had none of his own (he was indeed called John Lackland) he took it from the Saxons and gave it to the Normans. Thus many of the Saxons once more became homeless beggars, and lived a wild life in the forests, which covered a great part of England at this time.

Now among the few Saxon nobles who still remained, and who had not been robbed of their lands and money, there was one called Robert, Earl of Huntingdon. He had one son also named Robert, but people called him Robin. He was a favourite with every one. Tall, strong, handsome, and full of fun, he kept his father's house bright with songs and laughter. He was brave and fearless too, and there was no better archer in all the countryside. And with it all he was gentle and tender, never hurting the weak nor scorning the poor.

But Robert of Huntingdon had a bitter enemy. One day this enemy came with many soldiers behind him, determined to kill the earl and take all his goods and lands. There was a fierce and terrible fight, but in the end Robert and all his men were killed. His house was burned to the ground and all his money stolen. Only Robin was saved, because he was such a splendid archer that no soldier would go near him, either to kill him or take him prisoner. He fought bravely till the last, but when he saw that his father was dead and his home in flames, he had no heart to fight any longer. So taking his bow and arrows, he fled to the great forest of Sherwood.

Very fast he had to run, for Prince John's men were close behind him. Soon he reached the edge of the forest, but he did not stop there. On and on he went, plunging deeper and deeper under the shadow of the trees. At last he threw himself down beneath a great oak, burying his face in the cool, green grass.

His heart felt hot and bitter. He was full of rage and fierce thoughts of revenge. Cruel men in one day had robbed him of everything. His father, his home, servants, cattle, land, money, his name even, all were gone. He was bruised, hungry, and weary. Yet as he lay pressing his face against the cool, green grass, and clutching the soft, damp moss with his hands, it was not sorrow or pain he felt, but only a bitter longing for revenge.

The great, solemn trees waved gently overhead in the summer breeze, the setting sun sent shafts of golden light into the cool, blue shadows, birds sang their evening songs, deer rustled softly through the underwood, and bright-eyed squirrels leaped noiselessly from branch to branch. Everywhere there was calm and peace except in poor Robin's angry heart.

Robin loved the forest. He loved the sights and scents, and the sounds and deep silences of it. He felt as if it were a tender mother who opened her wide arms to him. Soon it comforted him, and at last the tears came hot and fast, and sobs shook him as he lay on the grass. The bitterness and anger had all melted out of his heart; only sorrow was left.

In the dim evening light Robin knelt bareheaded on the green grass to say his prayers. Then, still bareheaded, he stood up and swore an oath. This was the oath:—

> "I swear to honour God and the King,
> To help the weak and fight the strong,
> To take from the rich and give to the poor,
> So God will help me with His power."

Then he lay down on the grass under the trees with his good long bow beside him, and fell fast asleep.

And this is how Robin Hood first came to live in the Green Wood and have all his wonderful adventures.

II

THE MEETING OF ROBIN HOOD AND LITTLE JOHN

When Robin first came to live in Sherwood Forest he was rather sad, for he could not at once forget all he had lost. But he was not long lonely. When it became known that he had gone to live in the Green Wood, other poor men, who had been driven out of their homes by the Normans, joined him. They soon formed a band and were known as the "Merry Men."

Robin was no longer Robin of Huntingdon, but Robin of Sherwood Forest. Very soon people shortened Sherwood into Hood, though some say he was called Hood from the green hoods he and his men wore. How he came to have his name does not matter much. People almost forgot that he was really an earl, and he had become known, not only all over England, but in many far countries, as Robin Hood.

Robin Hood was captain of the band of Merry Men. Next to him came Little John. He was called Little John because he was so tall, just as Midge the miller's son was called Much because he was so small.

Robin loved Little John best of all his friends. Little John loved Robin better than any one else in all the world. Yet the first time they met they fought and knocked each other about dreadfully.

> "How they came acquainted, I'll tell you in brief,
> If you will but listen a while;
> For this very jest, among all the rest,
> I think it may cause you to smile."

It happened on a bright, sunshiny day in early spring. All through the winter Robin and his men had had a very dull time. Nearly all their fun and adventures happened with people travelling through the forest. As there were no trains, people had to travel on horseback. In winter the roads were so bad, and the weather so cold and wet, that most people stayed at home. So it was rather a quiet time for Robin and his men. They lived in great caves during the winter, and spent their time making stores of bows and arrows, and mending their boots and clothes.

This bright, sunshiny morning Robin felt dull and restless, so he took his bow and arrows, and started off through the forest in search of adventure.

He wandered on for some time without meeting any one. Presently he came to a river. It was wide and deep, swollen by the winter rains. It was crossed by a very slender, shaky bridge, so narrow, that if two people tried to pass each other on it, one would certainly fall into the water.

Robin began to cross the bridge, before he noticed that a great, tall man, the very tallest man he had ever seen, was crossing too from the other side.

"Go back and wait till I have come over," he called out as soon as he noticed the stranger.

The stranger laughed, and called out in reply, "I have as good a right to the bridge as you. *You* can go back till *I* get across."

This made Robin very angry. He was so accustomed to being obeyed that he was very much astonished too. Between anger and astonishment he hardly knew what he did.

He drew an arrow from his quiver and fitting it to his bow, called out again, "If you don't go back I'll shoot."

"If you do, I'll beat you till you are black and blue," replied the stranger.

> "Quoth bold Robin Hood, Thou dost prate like an ass,
> For, were I to bend my bow,
> I could send a dart quite through thy proud heart,
> Before thou couldst strike a blow."

"If I talk like an ass you talk like a coward," replied the stranger. "Do you call it fair to stand with your bow and arrow ready to shoot at me when I have only a stick to defend myself with? I tell you, you are a coward. You are afraid of the beating I would give you."

Robin was not a coward, and he was not afraid. So he threw his bow and arrows on the bank behind him.

"You are a big, boastful bully," he said. "Just wait there until I get a stick. I hope I may give you as good a beating as you deserve."

The stranger laughed. "I won't run away; don't be afraid," he said.

Robin Hood stepped to a thicket of trees and cut himself a good, thick oak stick. While he was doing this, he looked at the stranger, and saw that he was not only taller but much stronger than himself.

However that did not frighten Robin in the least. He was rather glad of it indeed. The stranger had said he was a coward. He meant to prove to him that he was not.

Back he came with a fine big stick in his hand and a smile on his face. The idea of a real good fight had made his bad temper fly away, for, like King Richard, Robin Hood was rather fond of a fight.

"We will fight on the bridge," said he, "and whoever first falls into the river has lost the battle."

"All right," said the stranger. "Whatever you like. I'm not afraid."

Then they fell to, with right good will.

It was very difficult to fight standing on such a narrow bridge. They kept swaying backwards and forwards trying to keep their balance. With every stroke the bridge bent and trembled beneath them as

Bang! smash! their blows fell fast and thick as if they had been threshing corn.

if it would break. All the same they managed to give each other some tremendous blows. First Robin gave the stranger such a bang that his very bones seemed to ring.

"Ah, ha!" said he, "I'll give you as good as I get," and crack he went at Robin's crown.

Bang, smash, crack, bang, they went at each other. Their blows fell fast and thick as if they had been threshing corn.

> "The stranger gave Robin a knock on the crown,
> Which caused the blood to appear,
> Then Robin enraged, more fiercely engaged,
> And followed with blows more severe.
>
> So thick and fast did he lay it on him,
> With a passionate fury and ire,
> At every stroke he made him to smoke,
> As if he had been all on fire."

When Robin's blows came so fast and furious, the stranger felt he could not stand it much longer. Gathering all his strength, with one mighty blow he sent Robin backwards, right into the river. Head over heels he went, and disappeared under the water.

The stranger very nearly fell in after him. He was so astonished at Robin's sudden disappearance that he could not think for a minute or two where he had vanished to. He knelt down on the bridge, and stared into the water. "Hallo, my good man," he called. "Hallo, where are you?"

He thought he had drowned Robin, and he had not meant to do that. All the same he could not help laughing. Robin had looked so funny as he tumbled into the water.

"I'm here," called Robin, from far down the river. "I'm all right. I'm just swimming with the tide."

The current was very strong and had carried him down the river a good way. He was, however, gradually making for the bank. Soon he caught hold of the overhanging branches of a tree and pulled himself out. The stranger came running to help him too.

"You are not an easy man to beat or to drown either," he said with a laugh, as he helped Robin on to dry land again.

"Well," said Robin, laughing too, "I must own that you are a brave man and a good fighter. It was a fair fight, and you have won the battle. I don't want to quarrel with you any more. Will you shake hands and be friends with me?"

"With all my heart," said the stranger. "It is a long time since I have met any one who could use a stick as you can."

So they shook hands like the best of friends, and quite forgot that a few minutes before they had been banging and battering each other as hard as they could.

Then Robin put his bugle horn to his mouth, and blew a loud, loud blast.

"The echoes of which through the valleys did ring,
At which his stout bowmen appeared,
And clothèd in green, most gay to be seen,
So up to their master they steered."

When the stranger saw all these fine men, dressed in green, and carrying bows and arrows, come running to Robin he was very much astonished. "O master dear, what has happened?" cried Will Stutely, the leader, as he ran up. "You have a great cut in your forehead, and you are soaked through and through," he added, laying his hand on Robin's arm.

"It is nothing," laughed Robin. "This young fellow and I have been having a fight. He cracked my crown and then tumbled me into the river."

When they heard that, Robin's men were very angry. "If he has tumbled our master into the river, we will tumble him in," said they. "We will see how he likes that," and they seized him, and would have dragged him to the water to drown him, but Robin called out, "Stop, stop, it was a fair fight. He is a brave man, and we are very good friends now."

Then turning to the stranger, Robin bowed politely to him, saying, "I beg you to forgive my men. They will not harm you now they know that you are my friend, for I am Robin Hood."

The stranger was very much astonished when he heard that he had actually been fighting with bold Robin Hood, of whom he had heard so many tales.

"If you will come and live with me and my Merry Men," went on Robin, "I will give you a suit of Lincoln green. I will teach you how to use bow and arrows as well as you use your good stick."

"I should like nothing better," replied the stranger. "My name is John Little, and I promise to serve you faithfully."

"John Little!" said Will Stutely laughing. "John Little! what a name for a man that height! John Little! why he is seven feet tall if he is an inch!"

Will laughed and laughed, till the tears ran down his face. He thought it was such a funny name for so big a man.

Robin laughed because Will laughed. Then John Little laughed because Robin laughed. Soon they were all laughing as hard as they could. The wind carried the sound of it away, till the folk in the villages round about said, "Hark, how Robin Hood and his Merry Men do laugh."

"Well," said Robin at last, "I have heard it said, 'Laugh and grow fat,' but if we don't get some dinner soon I think we will all grow very lean. Come along, my little John, I'm sure you must be hungry too."

"Little John," said Will Stutely, "that's the very name for him. We must christen him again, and I will be his godfather."

Back to their forest home they all went, laughing and talking as merrily as possible, taking John Little along with them. Dinner was waiting for them when they arrived. The head cook was looking anxiously through the trees saying, "I do wish Master Robin would come, or the roast venison will be too much cooked and the rabbits will be stewed to rags."

Just at that moment they appeared. The cook was struck dumb at the sight of the giant, stalking along beside Robin. "Where has master gotten that Maypole?" he said, laughing to himself, as he ran away to dish the dinner.

They had a very merry dinner. Robin found that John was not only a good fighter but that he had a wise head and a witty tongue. He was more and more delighted with his new companion.

But Will and the others had not forgotten that he was to be christened again. Seven of them came behind him, and in spite of all his kicking and struggling wrapped him up in a long, green cloak, pretending he was a baby.

It was a very noisy christening. The men all shouted and laughed. John Little laughed and screamed in turn, and kicked and struggled all the time.

"Hush, baby, hush," they said. But the seven foot baby wouldn't hush.

Then Will stepped up beside him and began to speak.

"This infant was called John Little, quoth he,
Which name shall be changed anon,

The words we'll transpose, so wherever he goes,
His name shall be called Little John."

They had some buckets of water ready. These they poured over poor Little John till he was as wet as Robin had been after he fell into the river. The men roared with laughter. Little John looked so funny as he rolled about on the grass, trying to get out of his long, wet, green robe. He looked just like a huge green caterpillar.

Robin laughed as much as any one. At last he said, "Now, Will, don't you think that is enough?"

"Not a bit," said Will. "You wouldn't let us duck him in the river when we had him there so we have brought the river to him."

At last all the buckets were empty, and the christening was over. Then all the men stood round in a ring and gave three cheers for Little John, Robin's new man.

"Then Robin he took the sweet pretty babe,
And clothed him from top to toe
In garments of green, most gay to be seen,
And gave him a curious long bow."

After that they sang, danced, and played the whole afternoon. Then when the sun sank and the long, cool shadows fell across the grass they all said "good night" and went off into their caves to sleep.

From that day Little John always lived with Robin. They became very, very great friends and Little John was next to Robin in command of the men.

> "And so ever after as long as he lived,
> Although he was proper and tall,
> Yet, nevertheless, the truth to express,
> Still Little John they did him call."

III

THE WEDDING OF ALLAN-A-DALE

One day when Robin was walking through the wood, he met a gay young knight. The knight was dressed in scarlet satin, and wore a hat decked with feathers. He held his head erect and walked with a light and joyous step. As he walked he sang a merry song.

Robin wondered who the knight could be, but he did not stop him as he had other business that morning.

The next day Little John and Much, the tallest and the shortest of Robin Hood's band, went for a walk. It was very funny to see these two together. Little John was seven feet high and very straight and strong. Much was scarcely five and very broad and dumpy.

As they walked along they met the very knight that Robin had seen the day before. But how different he looked! It was difficult to believe that he was the same man.

"The scarlet he wore the day before
It was clean cast away,
And ev'ry step he fetched a sigh,
Alack, and well a day."

He was dressed all in dull grey. His head hung down, and he moved his feet as if they were made of lead. So sad was he that he did not see Little John and Much until they were close upon him. Then he would have drawn his bow and arrows to shoot at them, but they were too quick for him. Seizing him by the arms they led him before Robin Hood, who was sitting under his great oak-tree.

Robin rose politely, bowed to him, and bade him welcome to the Green Wood. Then still very politely (for being a real earl, Robin was always very polite to people, though he did rob them) he asked if the stranger had any money to spare for Robin Hood and his Merry Men.

"I have no money, the young man said,
But five shillings, and a ring;
And that I have kept, this seven long years,
To have at my wedding."

When Robin heard that the knight was so poor, he was very sorry for him, and asked him to sit down and tell him how that was, and why he was so sad. So with many a sigh the poor young man told his tale.

"My name is Allan-a-Dale," he said. "Seven years ago I fell in love with the most beautiful lady in all the world. She loved me too and we were very happy. But her father was very angry. I was poor, and he said we were too young to marry. He promised, however, that if we would wait seven years and a day we should then be married. The seven years are over, and yesterday should have been our wedding day. I went to claim my bride. But alas! the old knight would scarcely speak to me. He said his daughter was not for such a poor man as I. To-morrow she is to be married to another. He is old and ugly, but he has a great deal of money. So I have lost my love, and my heart is broken."

Then poor Allan-a-Dale dropped his head in his hands and groaned aloud.

"Nay," said Robin, "do not grieve so. A maiden who thus changes her mind is not worth so much sorrow."

But Allan-a-Dale shook his head. "Alas!" he sighed, "she loves me still. It is the old knight, her father, who forces her to do this thing."

> "Then what wilt thou give to me, said Robin Hood,
> In ready gold or fee,
> To help thee to thy true love again.
> And deliver her unto thee?"

"Why," said Allan, "I have no gold. But if you bring my true love back to me, I swear to serve you faithfully for ever and a day. I cannot shoot so far or so straight as your good men, but I can make and sing sweet songs and play upon the harp."

Robin was very glad when he heard that. He clapped Allan on the shoulder and told him to cheer up, for, said he, "to-morrow is your wedding day." Then he asked how far it was to the church where this wedding was to take place. Allan told him it was to be at Dale Abbey, not much more than five miles distant.

Very early next morning Robin Hood rose. He dressed himself like an old harper, and taking a harp, set off for Dale Abbey. He left orders with Little John that he was to follow with twenty-four good men all dressed in Lincoln green. Also he was to bring with him Friar Tuck and Allan-a-dale.

When Robin Hood arrived at the door of the Abbey, whom should he meet but the Bishop of Hereford, all dressed in his fine robes and all ready to marry poor Lady Christabel to the old knight.

"What do you here, my good man?" said the Bishop.

"Why," replied Robin, "I am a minstrel. Hearing there was to be a great wedding to-day, I have come to see it. Afterwards I can make a song about it."

"That is well," said the Bishop, "I love the sound of the harp and you can play some sweet music to us."

"I should like to see the bride and bridegroom first, before I play any music," replied Robin. Then he went into the church, and sat down behind a big pillar not far from the altar.

Soon the wedding guests began to arrive. There were a great many lovely ladies in beautiful dresses. They came in, rustling in silk and laces, nodding and smiling to each other, fluttering and flitting about the aisles of the great, dimly-lit church, like pretty painted butterflies. Robin watched them beckoning and whispering to each other. Sometimes he could hear what they said.

"Poor girl," said one, "so young and pretty."

"And he so old and ugly."

"Not to say wicked."

"And she loves some one else, I hear."

"Yes, Allan-a-Dale."

"What! the handsome young man who sings so beautifully?"

"Then why does he not carry her off?"

"Oh, he is too poor."

"Oh, the pity of it!"

Robin was glad. From all he heard, he learned that every one in the church was sorry for poor Christabel.

At last the bridegroom came. Silence fell upon the church as he entered. Nothing was heard except the ring of his gold-headed cane on the flagstones, as he hobbled up the aisle. So old and ugly he was. Older and uglier even than Robin had expected. He was tricked out, too, in a suit of white satin which helped to make him look more aged and withered.

Suddenly there was a little stir at the great west door. All heads turned. The bride had arrived. A sigh of admiration passed through the crowd.

She was so beautiful. With slow and stately steps she came, leaning on her father's arm. Her face was sad, her eyes cast down. Pale as any lily, she came robed in shimmering white satin. Round her white throat and in her golden hair, wonderful pearls gleamed in the dim light. If the bridegroom was more ugly than Robin had expected, the bride was far more beautiful. Behind her came the little choir boys, dressed in red and white, singing a sweet bridal song.

They reached the altar rails, and the Bishop opened his book to begin the service.

At that moment Robin sprang from behind the pillar and stood beside the bride.

"Stop!" he cried, "I do not like this wedding. The bridegroom is too old and ugly for such a lovely bride."

The ladies screamed, and at once the whole church was in commotion.

"Who are you who thus disturbs the peace of our holy service?" asked the Bishop.

"I am Robin Hood," replied he, throwing off his disguise, and putting his horn to his lips.

"I am Robin Hood," replied he, throwing off his disguise and putting his horn to his lips.

When they heard that, every one stopped screaming, and pressed forward, trying to catch sight of the wonderful man of whom they had heard so much.

"Then four-and-twenty bowmen bold
Came leaping o'er the lea.
And when they came to the churchyard,
Marching all in a row,
The first man was Allan-a-Dale
To give bold Robin his bow."

"Now," said Robin, "seeing we have all come to church it is a pity there should be no wedding. Let the lady choose of all these fine men which she will have."

The Lady Christabel's face was no longer pale, but dainty pink like the inside of a shell. She raised her eyes and saw that Allan-a-Dale was standing beside her. She put out her hand timidly and slipped it into his. He clasped it and bent to kiss it tenderly. Then it was as if two red rose petals had fluttered to her cheeks. She was no longer like a lily, but a queen with head erect, and shining, happy eyes.

"Now," said Robin, "the lady has chosen. We can have the wedding. Sir Bishop, do thy duty."

"Nay, but I will not," said the Bishop. "It is the law that every one must be asked in church three times before they can be married. Therefore I will not."

"If you will not we must get some one else," said Robin. "Come along, Friar Tuck."

So Friar Tuck put on the Bishop's fine gown and took his big book, and every one laughed as he stepped to the rails of the altar, he looked so fat and jolly.

> "When Friar Tuck went to the quire
> The people began to laugh,
> He asked them seven times in the church
> Lest three times should not be enough."

Then when he had finished asking them seven times, he told the people gravely that they really must not laugh any more, that it was not at all the proper thing to do in church. But the people were all so glad for Christabel they really could not help it.

Then he began the marriage service. "Who gives this maiden to be married?"

"That do I," said Robin.

Christabel's father would have liked to cry out and stop the wedding, but he could not. Two of Robin's men held him tight and kept their hands over his mouth so that he could not make a sound. No one else in all the church wanted to stop it except the Bishop and the old knight. They were both so angry that they could not speak. Besides they were both so old and feeble that they could do nothing.

So Christabel and Allan-a-Dale were married and went to live with Robin Hood in Sherwood Forest.

The wedding was long talked about. The people who were there said it was the prettiest and the merriest wedding they had ever seen. And to this day, if you go to Derbyshire, you can still see the ruins of the great abbey in which it took place.

IV

ROBIN HOOD AND THE BUTCHER

The Sheriff of Nottingham hated Robin and would have been very glad if any one had killed him.

The Sheriff was a very unkind man. He treated the poor Saxons very badly. He often took away all their money, and their houses and left them to starve. Sometimes, for a very little fault, he would cut off their ears or fingers. The poor people used to go into the wood, and Robin would give them food and money. Sometimes they went home again, but very often they stayed with him, and became his men.

The Sheriff knew this, so he hated Robin all the more, and he was never so happy as when he caught one of Robin's men and locked him up in prison.

But try how he might, he could not catch Robin. All the same Robin used to go to Nottingham very often, but he was always so well disguised that the Sheriff never knew him. So he always escaped.

The Sheriff was too much afraid of him to go into the forest to try to take him. He knew his men were no match for Robin's. Robin's men served him and fought for him because they loved him. The Sheriff's men only served him because they feared him.

One day Robin was walking through the forest when he met a butcher.

This butcher was riding gaily along to the market at Nottingham. He was dressed in a blue linen coat, with leather belt. On either side of his strong grey pony hung a basket full of meat.

In these days as there were no trains, everything had to be sent by road. The roads were so bad that even carts could not go along them very much, for the wheels stuck in the mud. Everything was carried on horseback, in sacks or baskets called panniers.

The butcher rode gaily along, whistling as he went. Suddenly Robin stepped from under the trees and stopped him.

"What have you there, my man?" he asked.

"Butcher meat," replied the man. "Fine prime beef and mutton for Nottingham Market. Do you want to buy some?"

"Yes, I do," said Robin. "I'll buy it all and your pony too. How much do you want for it? I should like to go to Nottingham and see what kind of butcher I will make."

So the butcher sold his pony and all his meat to Robin. Then Robin changed clothes with him. He put on the butcher's blue clothes and leather belt, and the butcher went off in Robin's suit of Lincoln green, feeling very grand indeed.

Then Robin mounted his pony and off he went to Nottingham to sell his meat at the market.

When he arrived he found the whole town in a bustle. In those days there were very few shops, so every one used to go to market to buy and sell. The country people brought butter and eggs and honey to sell. With the money they got they bought platters and mugs, pots and pans, or whatever they wanted, and took it back to the country with them.

All sorts of people came to buy: fine ladies and poor women, rich knights and gentlemen, and humble workers, every one pushing and crowding together. Robin found it quite difficult to drive his pony through the crowd to the corner of the market place where the butchers had their stalls.

He got there at last, however, laid out his meat, and began to cry with the best of them.

"Prime meat, ladies. Come and buy. Cheapest meat in all the market, ladies. Come buy, come buy. Twopence a pound, ladies. Twopence a pound. Come buy. Come buy."

"What!" said every one, "beef at twopence a pound! I never heard of such a thing. Why it is generally tenpence."

You see Robin knew nothing at all about selling meat, as he never bought any. He and his men used to live on what they shot in the forest.

When it became known that there was a new butcher, who was selling his meat for twopence a pound, every one came crowding round his stall eager to buy. All the other butchers stood idle until Robin had no more beef and mutton left to sell.

As these butchers had nothing to do, they began to talk among themselves and say, "Who is this man? He has never been here before."

"Do you think he has stolen the meat?"

"Perhaps his father has just died and left him a business."

"Well, his money won't last long at this rate."

"The sooner he loses it all, the better for us. We will never be able to sell anything as long as he comes here giving away beef at twopence a pound."

"It is perfectly ridiculous," said one old man, who seemed to be the chief butcher. "These fifty years have I come and gone to Nottingham market, and I have never seen the like of it—never. He is ruining the trade, that's what he is doing.

They stood at their stalls sulky and cross, while all their customers crowded round Robin.

Shouts of laughter came from his corner, for he was not only selling beef and mutton, but making jokes about it all the time.

"I tell you what," said the old butcher, "it is no use standing here doing nothing. We had better go talk to him, and find out, if we can, who he is. We must ask him to come and have dinner with us and the Sheriff in the town-hall to-day." For on market days the butchers used to have dinner altogether in the town-hall, after market was over, and the Sheriff used to come and have dinner with them.

> "So, the butchers stepped up to jolly Robin,
> Acquainted with him for to be;
> Come, butcher, one said, we be all of one trade,
> Come, will you dine with me?"

"Thank you," said Robin. "I should like nothing better. I have had a busy morning and am very hungry and thirsty."

"Come along, then," said the butchers.

The old man led the way with Robin, and the others followed two by two.

As they walked along, the old butcher began asking Robin questions, to try and find out something about him.

"You have not been here before?" he said.

"Have I not?" replied Robin.

"I have not seen you, at least."

"Have you not?"

"You are new to the business?"

"Am I?"

"Well, you seem to be," said the old butcher, getting rather cross.

"Do I?" replied Robin laughing.

At last they came to the town-hall, and though they had talked all the time the old butcher had got nothing out of Robin, and was not a bit wiser.

The Sheriff's house was close to the town-hall, so as dinner was not quite ready all the butchers went to say "How do you do?" to the Sheriff's wife.

She received them very kindly, and was quite interested in Robin when she heard that he was the new butcher who had been selling such wonderfully cheap meat. Robin had such pleasant manners too, that she thought he was a very nice man indeed. She was quite sorry when the Sheriff came and took him away, saying dinner was ready.

"I hope to see you again, kind sir," she said when saying good-bye. "Come to see me next time you have meat to sell."

"Thank you, lady, I will not forget your kindness," replied Robin, bowing low.

At dinner the Sheriff sat at one end of the table and the old butcher at the other. Robin, as the greatest stranger, had the place of honour on the Sheriff's right hand.

At first the dinner was very dull. All the butchers were sulky and cross, only Robin was merry. He could not help laughing to himself at the idea of dining with his great enemy the Sheriff of Nottingham. And not only dining with him, but sitting on his right hand, and being treated as an honoured guest.

If the Sheriff had only known, poor Robin would very soon have been locked up in a dark dungeon, eating dry bread instead of apple pie and custard and all the fine things they were having for dinner.

However, Robin was so merry, that very soon the butchers forgot to be cross and sulky. Before the end of dinner all were laughing till their sides ached.

Only the Sheriff was grave and thinking hard. He was a greedy old man, and he was saying to himself, "This silly young fellow evidently does not know the value of things. If he has any cattle I might buy them from him for very little. I could sell them again to the butchers for a good price. In that way I should make a lot of money."

After dinner he took Robin by the arm and led him aside.

"See here, young man," he said, "I like your looks. But you seem new to this business. Now don't trust these men," pointing to the butchers. "They are all as ready as can be to cheat you. You take my advice. If you have any cattle to sell, come to me. I'll give you a good price."

"Thank you," said Robin, "it is most kind of you."

"Hast thou any horned beasts, the Sheriff then said,
Good fellow, to sell to me?
Yes, that I have, good master Sheriff,
I have hundreds two or three.

And a hundred acres of good free land,
if you please it for to see;
And I'll make you as good assurance of it,
As ever my father did me."

The Sheriff nearly danced for joy when he heard that Robin had so many horned cattle for sale. He had quite made up his mind that it would be easy to cheat this silly young fellow. Already he began to count the money he would make. He was such a greedy old man. But there was a wicked twinkle in Robin's eye.

"Now, young man, when can I see these horned beasts of yours?" asked the Sheriff. "I can't buy a pig in a poke, you know. I must see them first. And the land too, and the land too," he added, rubbing his hands, and jumping about in his excitement.

"The sooner the better," said Robin. "I start for home to-morrow morning. If you like to ride with me I will show you the horned beasts and the land too."

"Capital, capital," said the Sheriff. "To-morrow morning then, after breakfast, I go with you. And see here, young man," he added, catching hold of Robin's coat tails, as he was going away, "you won't go and sell to any one else in the meantime? It is a bargain, isn't it?"

"Oh, certainly. I won't even speak of it to any one," replied Robin; and he went away, laughing heartily to himself.

That night the Sheriff went into his counting-house and counted out three hundred pounds in gold. He tied it up in three bags, one hundred pounds in each bag.

"It's a lot of money," he said to himself, "a lot of money. Still I suppose, I must pay him something for his cattle. But it is a lot of money to part with," and he heaved a big sigh.

He put the gold underneath his pillow in case any one should steal it during the night. Then he went to bed and tried to sleep. But he was too excited; besides the gold under his pillow made it so hard and knobby that it was most uncomfortable.

At last the night passed, and in the morning

"The Sheriff he saddled his good palfrey,
　　And with three hundred pounds in gold
Away he went with bold Robin Hood,
　　His horned beasts to behold."

The sun shone and the birds sang as they merrily rode along. When the Sheriff saw that they were taking the road to Sherwood Forest, he began to feel a little nervous.

"There is a bold, bad man in these woods," he said. "He is called Robin Hood. He robs people, he—do you think we will meet him?"

"I am quite sure we won't meet him," replied Robin with a laugh.

"Well, I hope not, I am sure," said the Sheriff. "I never dare to ride through the forest unless I have my soldiers with me. He is a bold, bad man."

Robin only laughed, and they rode on right into the forest.

> "But when a little further they came,
> Bold Robin he chanced to spy
> An hundred head of good fat deer
> Come tripping the Sheriff full nigh.

"Look there," he cried, "look! What do you think of my horned beasts?"

"I think," said the Sheriff, in a trembling voice, "I think I should go back to Nottingham."

"What! and not buy any horned Cattle? What is the matter with them? Are they not fine and fat? Are they not a beautiful colour? Come, come, Sheriff, when you have brought the money for them too."

At the mention of money the Sheriff turned quite pale and clutched hold of his bags. "Young man," he said, "I don't like you at all. I tell you I want to go back to Nottingham. This isn't money I have in my bags, it is only pebble stones."

> "Then Robin put his horn to his mouth,
> And blew out blasts three;
> Then quickly and anon there came Little John,
> And all his company."

"Good morning, Little John," said Robin.

"Good morning, Master Robin," he replied. "What orders have you for to-day?"

"Well, in the first place I hope you have something nice for dinner, because I have brought the Sheriff of Nottingham to dine with us," answered Robin.

"Yes," said Little John, "the cooks are busy already as we thought you might bring some one back with you. But we hardly expected so fine a guest as the Sheriff of Nottingham," he added, making a low bow to him. "I hope he intends to pay honestly."

For that was Robin Hood's way, he always gave these naughty men who had stolen money from poor people a very fine dinner and then he made them pay a great deal of money for it.

The Sheriff was very much afraid when he knew that he had really fallen into the hands of Robin Hood. He was angry too when he thought that he had actually had Robin in his own house the day before, and could so easily have caught and put him in prison, if he had only known.

They had a very fine dinner, and the Sheriff began to feel quite comfortable and to think he was going to get off easily, when Robin said, "Now, Master Sheriff, you must pay for your dinner."

"Oh! indeed I am a poor man," said the Sheriff, "I have no money."

"No money! What have you in your saddle bags, then?" asked Robin.

"Only pebbles, nothing but pebbles, I told you before," replied the frightened Sheriff.

"Little John, go and search the Sheriff's saddle bags," said Robin.

Little John did as he was told, and counted out three hundred pounds upon the ground.

"Sheriff," said Robin sternly, "I shall keep all this money and divide it among my men. It is not half as much as you have stolen from them. If you had told me the truth about it, I might have given you some back. But I always punish people who tell lies. You have done so many evil deeds," he went on, "that you deserve to be hanged."

The poor Sheriff shook in his shoes.

"Hanged you should be," continued Robin, "but your good wife was kind to me yesterday. For her sake, I let you go. But if you are not kinder to my people I will not let you off so easily another time." And Robin called for the Sheriff's pony.

"Then Robin he brought him through the wood,
And set him on his dapple grey:
Oh, have me commended to your wife at home,
So Robin went laughing away."

V

ROBIN HOOD AND THE BISHOP

"Come, children all, and listen a while,
And a story to you I'll unfold;
I'll tell you how Robin Hood served the Bishop,
When he robbed him of his gold."

The Bishop of Hereford was very angry with Robin Hood for the trick he had played him at Allan-a-Dale's wedding. He was so angry that he would have been pleased if any one had caught or killed Robin. But no one did. The wicked people were nearly all afraid of Robin and his brave men. The people who were kind and good loved him.

One day the Bishop had to take a great deal of money to a monastery. A monastery is a large house in which a number of good men live together. In those days, however, the men who lived in the monasteries were not always good. Sometimes they were very wicked indeed.

To reach the monastery the Bishop had to pass through part of Sherwood Forest. He felt sure he would meet Robin Hood, so he gathered together all his servants, and as many soldiers as he could. He hoped either to kill Robin or to take him prisoner, and bring him to Nottingham to have him hanged there.

He hoped most to take him prisoner, because he knew his friend, the Sheriff of Nottingham, was Robin's greatest enemy, and had promised to give a large sum of money to any one who would take him prisoner.

It was a bright, sunshiny day in the middle of June when the Bishop set out. It was cool and shady under the great leafy trees of the forest. Wild roses and pink and white morning-glory trailed across the path. The banks and ditches were gay with bright yellow moneywort and tansy. Sweetbrier and honeysuckle scented the air. Birds sang and twittered in the branches, and all the world was full of beauty.

Into the still and peaceful forest rode the Bishop and his men. Soon the woody paths were filled with the noise of neighing and trampling horses. The clang of swords, and the clatter and jingle of steel harness and armour, frightened the deer in their lairs, and the birdies in their nests.

But it was a splendid sight to see all those bold soldiers in shining armour riding along. The Bishop rode in the middle of them, wearing a gorgeous robe, trimmed with lace, over his armour.

Robin loved to roam in the forest, and he would often leave his men and wander off by himself. This morning everything was so bright and beautiful that he went on and on, hearing nothing but the song of birds, seeing nothing but the trees and flowers.

Suddenly he saw the Bishop and his men riding down a wide forest path. They, too, saw him quite plainly, for he was standing right in the middle of the path, looking up into a tree, listening to a blackbird singing.

> "O what shall I do, said Robin Hood then,
> If the Bishop he doth take me?
> No Mercy he'll show unto me, I know,
> But hangèd I shall be."

One man singly, however brave he might be, could not fight against all these soldiers. Nor could Robin call his men by blowing on his horn, as he generally did, when he was in danger. They were so far away, that long before they could reach him, Robin knew that he would be killed or taken prisoner.

It was a dreadful moment. With wild shouts of triumph the Bishop and his men were riding down upon him. There was only one thing to do. And Robin did it. He ran away.

Fast and faster he ran, closely followed by the Bishop's men. In and out among the trees he went, twisting and turning. After him came the soldiers, shouting wildly. He led them to the thickest part of the wood. On they came, trampling down the ferns, and crushing the pretty wildflowers.

Closer and closer grew the trees; narrower and narrower the pathways. Horses stumbled over roots or trailing branches of ivy, sending their riders sprawling on the ground. There they lay, unable to rise, because of the weight of their armour. The overhanging branches of the trees caught others, and knocked them off their horses, which galloped away riderless and terrified far into the forest.

It was a mad and breathless chase. Robin knew every path and secret way in all the woods. The trees seemed to bend down to hide him as he passed, or spread out their tough roots to trip up the horses of the Bishop's men.

Robin's suit, too, of Lincoln green, was almost the colour of the leaves in summer, and that helped him. The men found it more and more difficult to follow, and at last they lost him altogether.

He could hear their shouts growing fainter and fainter in the distance, but still he ran on. He knew the danger was not yet over. In the very thickest part of the wood he came to an old woman's cottage. He often sent presents to this poor old woman, so he was sure she would help him.

Knocking loudly on the door, he called out, "Open, open quickly and let me in."

The old woman hobbled to the door and opened it as fast as she could.

> "Why, who art thou? said the old woman,
> Come tell to me for good.
> I am an outlaw as many do know,
> And my name is Robin Hood.
>
> And yonder's the Bishop and all his men;
> And if that I taken be,
> Then day and night he'll work me spite,
> And hangèd I shall be."

"Come in," said the old woman, plucking him by the sleeve. "Come in quickly."

Robin stepped into the house. The old woman shut and bolted the door after him.

"If you are really Robin Hood," said she, looking at him hard, "I'll do anything I can to hide you from the Bishop and his men."

"I swear to you, my good woman, that I am truly Robin Hood. If you help me, neither my men nor I will ever forget it."

"I believe you, sir, I believe you. You have an honest face," answered the old woman. "And I'm not likely to forget all the kindness I have had from you and your Merry Men. Why, no later than last Saturday night you sent me a pair of shoes and some fine woollen stockings. See," she added, putting out one foot, "I'm wearing the shoes at this very minute.

But haste ye lad, haste ye," she went on more quickly, "where will ye hide?"

"In your grey gown," said Robin with a laugh.

The old woman looked at him in astonishment. "In my grey gown?" she said.

"Yes," said Robin; "give me a grey dress and a big white cap like those you wear. Dressed in them I can go safely through the wood till I meet my men. If I do chance to come across the Bishop and his soldiers I will hobble along like any old woman, and they will never stop to look at me. Then do you put on my suit of Lincoln green. If the Bishop follows me here, as I think he will, he will mistake you for me. Let him take you prisoner, and do not be afraid, for my good fellows and I will soon be back to rescue you from him."

"Bless your life, sir, what a head you have," said the old woman laughing. "I doubt if my old mutch ever covered so great a wit before."

Then she hobbled off, to get the clothes for Robin, as fast as ever she could.

When he was dressed, she gave him a spindle and flax in one hand and a stout walking-stick in the other.

> "And when Robin was so arrayed,
> He went straight to his company;
> With his spindle and twine, he oft looked behind
> For the Bishop and his company."

Once he met several of the Bishop's men who were now scattered through the woods, hunting everywhere for him. But he bent his back and hobbled slowly along like a very old woman, muttering and mumbling to himself till they were out of sight. So he got safely past.

It took him a long time to get to where his own men were. For one thing he found it was very difficult to walk in a dress. On the other hand, he was afraid to go too fast in case he should be seen by any of the Bishop's people.

At last he got to the place where he had left his men. There stood Little John looking out for him.

Robin waved his stick and shouted, but he was so well disguised that even his great friend did not know him.

"Look at that queer creature," said Little John to Will Scarlet who stood beside him. "I believe it's a witch. I'll shoot an arrow at her and see."

Little John knew that if it was a witch she would mount upon her stick and fly away over the trees as soon as she saw the arrow coming, and he wanted to see her do it.

He laid an arrow to his bow, and was just going to shoot when Robin cried out, "Stop, stop, Little John. It is Robin Hood."

Little John threw down his bow, and ran to him calling out, "Master, master, I might have shot you. What has happened that you come back in this guise?"

Robin soon told all his tale. Then said, "Now gather all our men, for we must fight the Bishop and save this good old woman."

Very soon, Robin, once more dressed in Lincoln green, was marching gaily at the head of his men, through the forest, searching for the Bishop and his company.

The old woman had barely had time to get into Robin's clothes before the Bishop arrived. He was pretty sure that Robin would take refuge in her cottage.

> "So the Bishop he came to the old woman's house,
> And he called with furious mood;,
> Come let me soon see, and bring unto me
> That traitor Robin Hood."

The old woman said never a word. She let them shout and bang at her door as much as they liked. With Robin's hat pulled well down over her face, she stood in a dark corner and waited. After a great deal of noise, they burst the door open and rushed in. They shouted with triumph when they saw the figure in green standing in the corner.

The old woman had armed herself with a good stout stick. With this she laid about her making a great show of fighting. She did indeed give one or two of the Bishop's men hearty smacks on the head. The noise was tremendous. Outside she could hear the Bishop shouting, "Gently, my men, gently. Take him alive, take him alive."

After a little she pretended to give in, and allowed several of the men to tie her hands behind her back. They led her out to the Bishop. So glad was he to see Robin Hood, as he thought, captured and bound, that he rocked in his saddle for very joy.

"Aha, my man," he cried, "we have you at last. Say farewell to your Green Wood. You will never see it again."

The old woman held her head down, though her hat was pulled well over her face, for fear the Bishop would find out that she was not Robin Hood at all.

But the Bishop was so old and blind that he could not tell that it was not Robin. Besides, he was so sure that he had got him that he hardly even looked at the old woman's face. He thought Robin was hanging his head in shame.

"Ho there," he cried, "honour to the prince of thieves. The finest horse in the company for the King of Sherwood Forest."

So a milk-white horse, the finest in all the company, was brought forward. Two men helped the old woman on to it. They tied her on firmly in case she should try to jump off and run away.

"He is ugly enough anyhow," said one man, looking at the old woman.

"As ugly as sin," said another.

"Ah, my children," said the Bishop, who heard them, "you see what sin does. This man leads a wicked life, and it has left its mark on his face."

When the old woman heard that, she shook with anger. It was so untrue.

The Bishop thought that Robin was trembling in fear. "Ah, you may well tremble my man," he said. "The punishment of all your wicked deeds is near." But the old woman never answered a word.

"Sound the trumpet," said the Bishop turning to the captain of his soldiers. "Call in all our scattered men, for I would be at St. Mary's Abbey by noon."

So the trumpet was sounded, and all the Bishop's servants and soldiers gathered together again. Once more they set off, the old woman on her beautiful white horse riding beside the Bishop on his dapple grey pony.

As they rode along the Bishop laughed and sang for joy. He was so glad that he had taken Robin Hood prisoner. His laughter did not last long, however.

"For as they were riding the forest along,
The Bishop chanced to see
A hundred brave bowmen stout and strong
Stand under the Green Wood Tree."

"Who are these," said the Bishop, "and what man is that who leads them?"

Then for the first time the old woman spoke. "Faith," said she, "I think it is a man called Robin Hood."

The Bishop made his pony stop, and laying a hand on the old woman's reins turned to her with a pale face. "Who are you, then?" he asked.

"Only an old woman, my Lord Bishop. Only an old woman and not Robin Hood at all," she replied.

> "Then woe is me, the Bishop said,
> That ever I saw this day!
> He turned him about, but Robin so stout,
> Called to him and bid him to stay."

"No, my Lord Bishop," said Robin, taking his hat off and bowing politely, "no, my lord, you cannot go yet. You owe us something for all the trouble you have given us."

Then he went to the old woman, unbound her hands, and lifted her gently to the ground. "I thank you, dame," he said, "for your kindness to me this day. Robin Hood will never forget it. Now you must have more comfortable clothes. If you follow Much the Miller's son he will take you to Maid Marian. She is waiting for you."

"No, my Lord Bishop," said Robin, "you cannot go yet."

"Thank you kindly," said the old woman, as she went away laughing, "but I think I'll take to wearing Lincoln green myself."

The Bishop's men did not attempt to fight. They saw it was useless. Robin had gathered so many of his brave men that they could easily have killed all the Bishop's men if they had tried. So they laid down their swords and spears and waited quietly to see what would happen next.

> "Then Robin took hold of the Bishop's horse,
> And tied him fast to a tree;
> Then smiled Little John his master upon,
> For joy of his company."

Robin then helped the Bishop to get off his horse, and gave him a comfortable seat on the root of a tree. Then seating himself opposite he said, "Now, my Lord Bishop, how much money have you with you?"

"The money which I have with me is not mine," replied the Bishop.

"Very true it is not yours," agreed Robin smiling.

"It belongs to the monastery of St. Mary," said the Bishop.

"Pardon me, it belongs to the poor people from whom you have stolen it," said Robin sternly, "to whom it is now going to be returned. Little John, bring the Bishop's money bags."

Little John brought the Bishop's money bags and counted out five hundred pounds upon the ground.

"Now let him go," said Robin.

"Master," said Little John, "it is a long time since I have heard High Mass sung, or indeed since we have had any service except what Friar Tuck gives us. May the Bishop not sing Mass before he goes?"

"You are right," said Robin, gravely rising and laying his hand on Little John's arm. "I have to-day much to be thankful for. The Bishop shall sing Mass before he goes."

So in the dim wood, beneath the tall trees which formed an archway overhead, as if they had been in a great cathedral, Robin and his men, and the Bishop and his men, friend and foe, knelt together side by side while the Bishop sang Mass. The birds joined in the singing and the trees whispered the amens.

Then Robin called for the Bishop's pony. He set him on it and led him and his men back to the broad path through the woods.

There he took leave of them. "Go," he said to the Bishop, "thank God for all His mercies to you this day, and in your prayers forget not Robin Hood."

VI

ROBIN HOOD AND MAID MARIAN

"A bonny fine maid of noble degree,
Maid Marian called by name,
Did live in the north, of excellent worth,
For she was a gallant dame.

For favour, and face, and beauty most rare,
Queen Helen she did excel;
For Marian then was praised of all men
That did in the country dwell."

Long before Robin came to live in Sherwood Forest he used often to go there to hunt. There were many wild animals in the woods which people were allowed to shoot. Only the deer belonged to the king, and no one was allowed to hunt or kill them.

One day while Robin was hunting in the forest he met a most beautiful lady. She was dressed in green velvet, the colour of the grass in spring. Robin thought she looked like a queen. He had never seen any one so lovely.

"Her gait it was graceful, her body was straight,
And her countenance free from all pride;
A bow in her hand, and a quiver of arrows,
Hung dangling down by her side.

Her eyebrows were black, ay, and so was her hair,
And her skin was as smooth as glass;
Her visage spoke wisdom and modesty too:
Suits with Robin Hood such a lass!"

Robin watched this beautiful lady shooting, and thought he had never seen anything so fine in all his life. He loved her from the very first moment he saw her.

"Oh, how sweet it would be if this dear lady would be my bride," he sighed to himself, though he did not even know her name.

He soon found that she was called Marian, and that her father was the noble Earl of Fitzwalter, who had come to live at a castle not far from his own home.

After this, Marian and Robin met each other very often. They used to hunt together in the forest, and came to love one another very much indeed. They loved each other so much, that Robin asked Marian to marry him, so that they might never be parted any more.

Marian said "yes," and Robin thought he was the happiest man in all the world. She went back to her own home with her father, to prepare for the wedding, which was to be in a few days. But just then a terrible misfortune happened to Robin. He lost his home, and everything that he had.

> "So fortune bearing these lovers a spite,
> Thus soon they were forced to part;
> To the merry Green Wood went Robin Hood
> With a sad and sorrowful heart."

When Robin lost all his money and lands, and had no house but only the Green Wood to live in, he said: "I cannot ask a gentle lady to come and live this rough life with me. I must say good-bye to my dear Marian for ever."

So he wrote a sad letter, telling her of all the terrible misfortune that had befallen him. "I shall love you always," he said, "but this life is too hard for a sweet and gentle lady, so I will never see you more. Good-bye."

Marian was very, very sorrowful when she had read Robin's letter. She cried all day long as if her heart would break.

She was very sad and lonely now, and all the world seemed dark and dreary. It seemed as if the sun had forgotten to shine and the birds to sing.

At last she became so miserable that she could bear it no longer. "I must go into the Green Wood and look for Robin," she said. "Perhaps if I see him again the pain will go out of my heart and the weariness from my feet."

It was a long way to Sherwood Forest. Marian knew that it was not safe for a beautiful lady to travel so far by herself. She feared the robbers and the wild, wicked men she might meet. So she dressed herself like a knight all in shining armour. She wore a steel helmet, with a white feather as a crest. Over her lovely face she drew a steel chain cover, called a visor, which knights used to wear. It kept the face from being hurt by arrows and swords in battle, and also, if a knight wished not to be known, it prevented people from seeing his face altogether.

> With quiver and bow, sword, buckler, and all,
> Thus armed was Marian most bold,
> She wandered about, to find Robin out,
> Whose person was better than gold."

Robin was very fond of disguising himself. He was very clever at it too. Often his dearest friends could not recognise him when they met him dressed like some one else.

One day he dressed himself as a Norman knight, pulled his visor over his face, and went out into the forest in search of an adventure.

He had not gone far before he met another knight in shining armour and a white crest. He put on a deep and terrible voice and called out in Norman French, "Stop, Sir knight of the white feather. No one passes through the forest without leave from me. I give leave only to those whose errand is good and whose name is fair. What is your name and where are you going?"

Marian (for of course it was she) was very frightened. Robin's voice sounded so gruff and terrible that she did not know it, and she could not see his face.

She thought he was some wicked Norman knight. Without saying a word she drew her sword and prepared to fight.

"Ah," said Robin, "you refuse to answer. Your errand must be evil if you cannot tell what it is. Fight then, false knight."

He too drew his sword, and the fight began. Though Robin was taller and stronger than Marian, she used her sword so cleverly, that he found it hard to get the better of her. He could not but admire the skill and grace with which she defended herself. "It is wonderful that a knight so young and so slender should have such strength and quickness," he said to himself. "I would he were one of my men."

They fought for more than an hour. Marian was wounded in the arm. Robin had a cut in his cheek, where the point of her sword had pierced his visor. Marian was growing tired. Robin began to feel sorry for the young knight who fought so skilfully and well.

"Oh, hold thy hand, hold thy hand, said Robin Hood,
And thou shalt be one of my string,
To range in the wood with bold Robin Hood
And hear the sweet nightingale sing."

Robin had forgotten that he was pretending to be a haughty Norman knight, and spoke in his own voice. When Marian heard it she dropped her sword with a cry of delight. "Robin, Robin," was all she could say.

"Marian," he replied full of wonder, "Marian can it be you? Oh, why did you not speak before? I have hurt you," he added in great distress. Marian took off her helmet so that he might see it was indeed his own true love. Her face was pale, but there was a smile on her lips, and her eyes were full of happy tears.

How they laughed and cried, and kissed each other. It was a long, long time since they had met. They went to the brook, which gurgled and sang through the wood not far off. Very tenderly Robin bathed and bound up Marian's wound, and she as gently cared for his. All the time they laughed and talked, and Marian found that the pain had gone from her heart and the weariness from her feet.

She told Robin how sad and sorrowful she had been, and how she had put on a knight's armour, and come to look for him.

"Sweetheart," he said when she had finished her story, "I do not know how I shall live in the Green Wood when you go away again."

"But I never mean to go away again. I am going to stay with you always," she said.

"Dearest, you must not. It is a rough, uncomfortable life, not fit for a gentle lady like you."

"Oh Robin, do not be so unkind. The sun does not shine and the birds forget to sing when I am away from you. Let me stay."

So Robin let her stay. He wanted to have her with him so much that he could not say "no" when she begged so hard.

"And then as bold Robin Hood, and his sweet bride,
Went hand and hand to the green bower,
The birds sung with pleasure in merry Sherwood,
And twas a joyful hour."

As they walked along to the Trysting-Tree, as the place was called where Robin and his men used to gather, they met Little John. He was very much surprised to see his master and a strange young knight, walking arm-in-arm, chatting and laughing gaily.

"Ho, Little John," called out Robin, as soon as he saw him, "come, help me. This fair knight has pierced my heart, so that I fear I shall never recover."

Little John turned pale. "Master," he said, "are you indeed wounded? If it is so, this false knight has not long to live," and he looked fiercely at Marian.

She drew closer to Robin, saying, "This big man frightens me."

But Robin laughed. Putting one arm round her, and holding Little John off with the other, "Friend," he said, "I did but jest. This is no knight, but my own fair love, Maid Marian. If my heart is pierced and sore wounded, it is only with the bright glances from her eyes. Marian," he went on, "this is my friend Little John, of whom I have told you. He is the tallest and the bravest of my men, the wisest head among us."

Little John knelt on one knee, and, taking Marian's hand, kissed it as if she had been a queen. "Lady," he said, "if you have come to live with us in the Green Wood, and be our queen, as Robin is our king, I swear to serve you faithfully and well, as I do him."

Marian smiled down upon him. Her heart was so full, she could not speak.

"Now, master," said Little John, "we must have a feast to-day, for this must be a great day in the Green Wood. So by your leave I will take my bow and arrows, and see what I can bring to our cooks."

"So Little John took his bow in his hand,
And wandered in the wood,
To kill the deer, and make a good cheer
For Marian and Robin Hood."

"Robin," said Marian, when Little John had gone, "I wish I had a dress to wear instead of this armour."

"Sweetheart," replied Robin, "you are lovely as you are, but if you want a dress you can soon have one. Not long ago we stopped a rich Jew, who was travelling through the forest. He left a bale of goods with us. There are several fine dresses in it, of which you can take your choice. Come, I will show you the cave where they are."

Robin sat down outside the cave to wait till Marian came back to him again. He leaned his head against the trunk of a tree, and shutting his eyes, dreamed happy day dreams.

Then he heard his name whispered, and, opening his eyes, saw Marian, looking like a fairy princess. She wore an underdress of glittering white, and over it a robe of lovely satin, green and shimmering like beech leaves in early spring. Her dark hair was caught up in a net of pearls, and a soft white veil fell about her face.

Robin drew in his breath. He had not known that any one could look so beautiful.

Slowly they paced through the Green Wood together. They had so much to say to each other, the time went all too quickly.

Then, under the Trysting-Tree, Robin stopped, and blew his horn. In answer to it all, all his men came marching in a row. As they passed Robin, every man bowed. Then each one knelt on one knee, kissing Marian's hand, and vowing to serve and honour her as his queen. And so every man went to his place, and Marian stood blushing and smiling at them as they passed.

Slowly they paced through the Green Wood.

Then the merry feast began. The cooks had done their very best, and had made all the most dainty and delightful dishes they could think of. The table-cloths, which were spread upon the grass, were strewn with wildflowers. The sun shone, the birds sang, and happy talk and laughter rang merrily through the wood.

When the feast was over, Robin filled his drinking-horn, and holding it high above his head said, "Here's a health to Maid Marian, Queen of the Green Wood."

It was a fine sight to see all his men as they sprang to their feet. They looked so handsome and tall in their coats of Lincoln green. They waved their hats and cheered for Maid Marian, till the forest echoed again.

"Here's to fair Maid Marian and bold Robin Hood," they cried. "Long may they live, and happy may they be."

Then came fat and jolly Friar Tuck carrying his big book and trying to look grave.

A hush fell upon every one, while Robin and Marian knelt together, under the blue sky and green waving branches. Very solemn and still it was, in the great forest, as Robin and Marian were married.

"Then a garland they brought her, by two and by two,
And placed it all on the Bride's head.
Then music struck up, and they all fell to dance,
And the Bride and Bridegroom they led."

Every one was happy and merry. Only Little John felt the least bit sad. "Now Robin has such a lovely wife, he will not need his friends any more," he said sorrowfully to himself.

But Maid Marian saw that he looked sad, and guessed why, so she talked kindly to him, and soon he was as merry as the rest. They sang, and danced, and played, and no one seemed to tire.

> "At last they ended their merriment,
> And went to walk in the wood,
> When Little John on Maid Marian
> Attended and bold Robin Hood."

So this happy day came to an end. The red sun sank behind the trees. The birds slept, and all the forest was silent, only the bright stars were awake, and watched over Robin and his band.

Robin and Marian lived together for a long, long time, and were very, very happy. They lived so happily together, and loved each other so much, that "to love like Robin Hood and Maid Marian" came to be a proverb. And to this day, in the place where Maid Marian lived before she went to the Green Wood, and where she was buried when she died, they give a prize each year to the man and wife who have lived most happily together.

> "In solid content together they lived
> With all their yeomen gay,
> They lived by their hands without any lands,
> And so they did many a day."

VII

ROBIN HOOD AND THE SILVER ARROW

Over and over again the Sheriff of Nottingham tried to catch Robin Hood. Over and over again he failed. Each time he failed he grew more angry, till wicked anger filled all his heart, and he could think of nothing else.

At last he said to himself, "I will go to the King, and ask him to give me a great many soldiers, so that I can fight, Robin and his men, and kill them all."

King Richard had come back from the Holy Land, because, even far off there, he had heard of the wicked things Prince John was doing.

So one fine day the Sheriff of Nottingham set out for London to visit the King. It took him many days to reach London, for as there were no trains, he had to ride all the way. He took a great many servants with him, and soldiers too, in case they should meet any robbers on the road.

Late one evening he arrived in London, very tired indeed with his long journey.

Next day, after he had rested a little, he put on his best clothes. He put a thick gold chain round his neck and a lovely red cloak over his shoulders. He looked very fine indeed. Then he set off to visit the King in his palace.

There he told all his tale—how Robin robbed the rich and haughty Norman nobles, helped the poor Saxons, and, above all, how he killed and ate the King's deer in Sherwood Forest.

"Why, and what shall I do?" said the King. "Are you not Sheriff? Are there no laws? If you cannot make people keep the laws or punish them when they break them, you are no good Sheriff. Go back to Nottingham, and if, when I come, I find that you have not kept good order, and acted justly, I will take away your office and give it to a better man."

So the Sheriff returned home very sad indeed. Instead of giving him any help the King had been angry with him. What made him saddest was the thought of all the money he had spent in going to London. For the Sheriff of Nottingham was a greedy old man. He loved money almost as much as he hated Robin Hood.

All the long way home he kept thinking and thinking how he might get Robin into his power. At last he fell upon a plan.

He thought he would have a beautiful silver arrow made with a golden head. This arrow he would offer as a prize to the man who could shoot best. He knew Robin and his men would hear about this shooting-match, and would come to try to win the prize. He meant to have a great many soldiers ready, and, as soon as Robin and his men came into the town, the soldiers would seize them and put them into prison.

Long ago when people went to battle they had no guns or cannons. Instead, they fought with swords and spears, or bows and arrows. The English archers, as the men who used bows and arrows were called, were the best in all the world. They could shoot further and straighter than any one else. And of all the English archers Robin Hood was the best. He could shoot further and straighter than any one in the whole world.

As soon as the Sheriff arrived home he sent for a man who made arrows. He told him to make the most beautiful arrow that had ever been seen, as he was going to have a grand shooting-match, and must have a very splendid prize.

Then he sent messengers into the towns and villages round to tell all the archers about it. Next he sent for the captain of his soldiers. He told him that he hoped to seize Robin Hood at the shooting-match, and that he must gather together as many soldiers as he could. "We must have two for every one of Robin Hood's men," he said. "There must be no mistake this time."

Everything was arranged and the day fixed.

Among Robin's men there was a brave young man called David of Doncaster. He had not been very long with Robin, and had a sister who lived in

Nottingham, and who was a servant in the Sheriff's house.

David often used to disguise himself and go into Nottingham to see his sister. One day she met him with a pale face. "David," she said, "you must not come here any more. Go, tell your master Robin Hood that the Sheriff means to kill him and all his men at the great shooting-match."

"What shooting-match?" asked David.

"Oh, have you not heard?" said his sister. "There is to be a great shooting-match next Tuesday. The prize is a silver arrow tipped with gold. But it is all a trick of the Sheriff's to get hold of Robin Hood. I heard him talking about it to the captain of the soldiers last night."

"Good-bye," said David, "I must go back to the forest to warn Robin as quickly as possible."

When he got back to the Green Wood he found that the news of the match had reached Robin. The men were all gathered together talking it over, and already preparing their bows and arrows.

"With that stepped forth the brave young man,
David of Doncaster:
Master, he said, be ruled by me,
From the Green Wood we'll not stir;

To tell the truth, I'm well informed
This match it is a wile;
The Sheriff, I wiss, devises this,
Us archers to beguile."

"You talk like a coward," said Robin. "If you are afraid, stay home with the women. As for me, I intend to try for this prize." Robin was so brave, that it made him careless of danger, and often led him into doing foolish things.

David was hurt that Robin should call him a coward, so he turned away without another word.

But in a minute Robin was sorry for what he had said. "Ho there! David," he called out. "I didn't mean it, my lad. Come back and tell us what you have heard."

When David had told them all he knew, they agreed that it would never do to walk straight into the trap which the Sheriff had prepared for them.

"Yet I should dearly like to go," said Robin.

"Well I don't see why we should not," said Little John. "Of course it would be very foolish to go as we are, dressed in Lincoln green. But why should we not all leave off our Lincoln green for one day, and dress ourselves each as differently as possible? No one would notice us then. We could go and come quite safely.

"One shall wear white, another red,
One yellow, another blue,
Thus in disguise, to the exercise
We'll gang, whate'er ensue."

"That is a very good plan," said Robin. "Do you not think so, David?" he added, laying a hand upon his shoulder, for he wanted to make David forget his unkind words.

"Why, yes, master, I think it will be very good fun," replied David, laughing, for he was very good tempered as well as brave, and had quite forgiven Robin already. "May I come too?"

"Yes, lad," said Robin. "You shall come with me. For we must not go all together," he continued, turning to the men. "We must go in twos and threes, and mix with the other people, or the Sheriff will soon guess who we are in spite of our clothes."

So it was all settled. The men had a merry time dressing up and arranging what they were to wear. Early on Tuesday morning they set off in twos and threes, going to Nottingham by different roads. They were soon lost among the crowds, who were all making their way to the place where the match was to be. All sorts of people were hurrying along, some to try for the prize, others to look on. Men, women, and children, old and young, rich and poor, were there. Every one had a holiday, even the schoolgirls and boys, and dressed in their best, they were all crowding along towards Nottingham.

From a window in his house the Sheriff kept looking and looking for Robin and his men, but no Lincoln green could he see. He was dreadfully disappointed. He kept saying to himself, "Surely he will come yet. Surely he will come."

The man who kept order and arranged everything about the match, and who was called the Master of the Lists, came to him and said, "Will you come now please, your honour, for it is time the match began? Every one is waiting for you and your lady."

"How many men have come to try for the prize?" asked the Sheriff.

"About eight hundred," replied the Master of the Lists.

"Is Robin Hood there, and any of his men, think you?"

"Nay," said the Master of the Lists, shaking his head, "not a man of his. There are many strangers, and a good number of King's foresters, but not a man in the Lincoln green of Robin Hood."

The Sheriff sighed. "He will surely come," he said. "Wait but a few minutes yet."

So the Master of the Lists waited for a few minutes. Then he came again to the Sheriff, and said, "We must indeed begin now. The people grow impatient. There are so many men to try for the prize, that if we do not begin at once, we cannot finish to-day."

"I suppose we must begin," sighed the Sheriff. "But I thought he would surely come."

He gave his wife his arm, and they took the seats of honour prepared for them, just behind where the archers stood to shoot their arrows.

Then the match began. It was a fine sight. The open space where it took place was like a great plain. At one end were set up fifty targets for the men to shoot at. These were painted different colours. The very middle of the target was painted white. Then came a red ring, then a black one, and last a yellow one.

At the opposite end of the plain, or lists as it was called, stood the archers. They had to try to send their arrows right into the middle of the target, and hit the white spot.

It was very exciting. All round, the people stood or sat, watching. Whenever any one hit the white, they cheered loudly. If any one missed the target altogether, they groaned. Those who missed the target were not allowed to shoot any more. The man who hit the white most often won the prize.

Robin and his men shot splendidly. Every time, Robin sent his arrow right into the very middle of the white part. His men sometimes hit the white, sometimes the red, but never got so far away from the middle of the target as the black or yellow.

"Some said, if Robin Hood was here,
And all his men to boot,
Sure none of them could pass these men,
So bravely they do shoot.

Ay, quoth the Sheriff, and scratched his head,
I thought he would have been here;
I thought he would, but though he's bold
He durst not now appear."

Robin had just been shooting. He was standing very close to where the Sheriff and his wife were sitting, and heard what the Sheriff said. It made him quite angry to think that any one would believe that he and his men had been frightened away. He longed to tell the Sheriff there and then that Robin Hood was standing beside him. He made up his mind to win the prize, and to let the Sheriff know somehow or other that he had done so.

The shooting went on, and the people grew more and more excited.

"Some cried Blue jacket, another cried Brown,
And the third cried Brave Yellow,
But the fourth man said, Yon man in Red
In this place has no fellow."

The man in red was Robin Hood himself. The man they called Brave Yellow was no other than brave David of Doncaster, who had shot nearly as well as Robin Hood.

At last the shooting came to an end. Of course Robin had won the prize. The people cheered loudly when he went up to the Sheriff's wife, who presented him with the arrow. She made a pretty little speech to him, and he thanked her politely, as he always did.

Then every one went home again. Robin and his men went back as they had come, by twos and

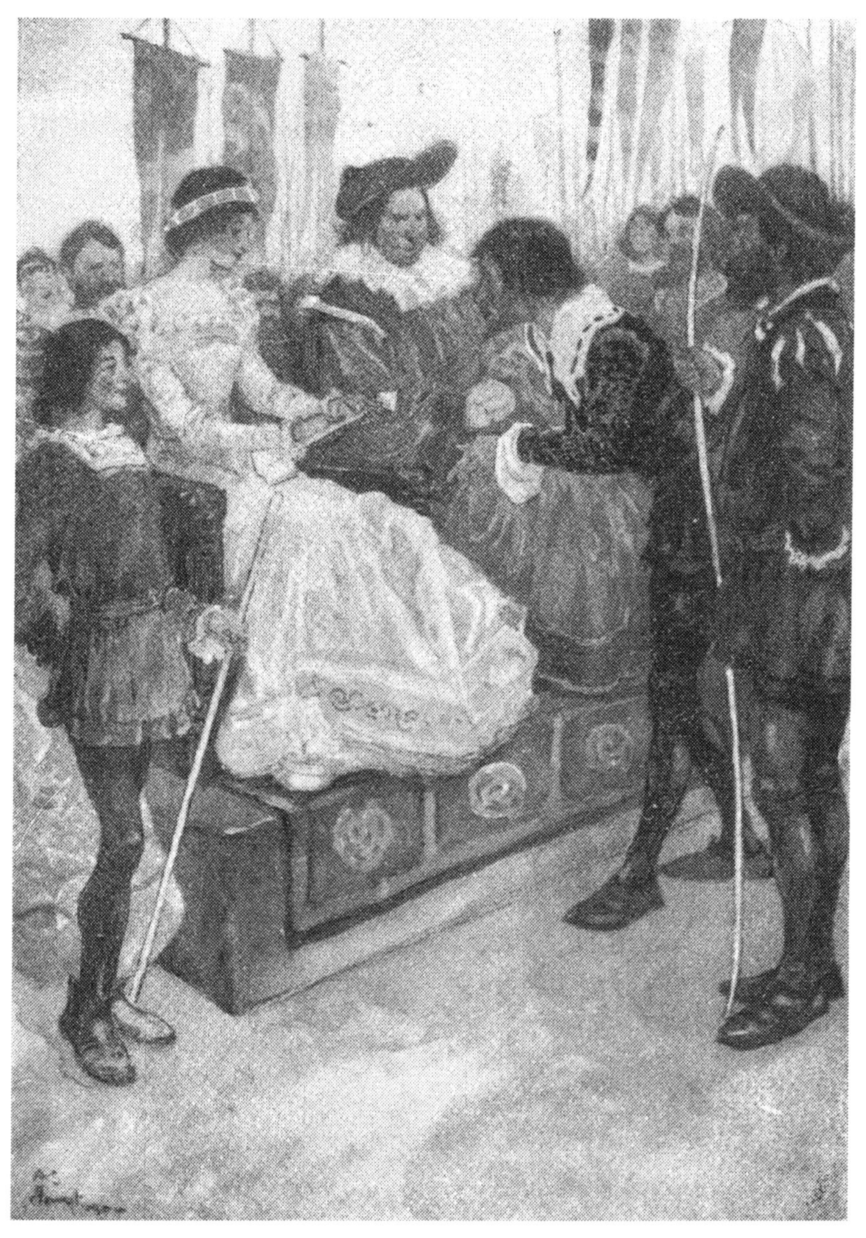

The Sheriff's wife, who presented him with the arrow

threes, and by different roads, so no one suspected who they were, least of all the Sheriff.

That night the Sheriff's wife said to him, "What a nice-looking man that was who won the prize to-day. How well he shot too! I have never seen anything like it. Do you know, he reminded me very much of that pleasant young butcher you brought to see me some time ago."

"Eh! What!" said the Sheriff, "I hope not. I most sincerely hope not." The Sheriff had never dared to tell his wife that the pleasant butcher man was really Robin Hood.

When Robin and his men were all met again under the Green Wood Tree, they had a merry time. There was a grand supper waiting for them. Such laughing and talking there was; they had so many adventures to relate, such jokes to tell. The beautiful silver arrow was passed round, and every one admired it very much.

> "Says Robin Hood, All my care is
> How that yon Sheriff may
> Know certainly that it was I
> That bore his arrow away."

Then Little John said, "You took my advice about going to the match, perhaps you will let me give you a little more."

"Speak on, speak on, said Robin Hood,
Thy wit's both quick and sound;
I know no man amongst us can
For wit like thee be found."

"I advise you then," said Little John, "to write a letter to the Sheriff. Tell him that we were all there, and that you were the man in red who carried off the prize. Then when you have written the letter, send it to Nottingham."

"Very good advice," replied Robin; "but how are we going to send it? Our messenger could not get out of the town before the Sheriff had read the letter. He would certainly send after him to seize him and shut him up in prison. I cannot allow any of my men to put himself in danger for a mere whim of mine."

In those days, you see, there were no posts, or postmen. If you wanted to send a letter to any one, you had to pay a special messenger to carry it for you. It cost a great deal, so people hardly ever wrote letters at all. Indeed, very many people could neither read nor write them.

"Pugh!" said Little John, in answer to Robin, "it is easy enough. Write your letter, address it to the Sheriff, and I will stick it on to the end of an arrow, and shoot it into the town."

"Bravo! Bravo!" shouted every one. "Hurrah for Little John, clever Little John."

"The project it was well performed:
The Sheriff the letter had,
Which, when he read, he scratched his head,
And raved like one that's mad."

VIII

ROBIN HOOD AND KING RICHARD

"King Richard hearing of the pranks
Of Robin Hood and his men,
He much admired, and more desired
To see both him and them."

When Richard Cœur de Lion came back from the Holy Land, he found England in a sad state. Prince John had ruled very badly and had done many cruel and unjust acts. He had made the people very unhappy, so they rejoiced greatly when the King returned.

He set to work at once to try to put things right again. After he had been in London a short time, he decided to go to Nottingham to find out for himself the truth about Robin Hood.

With a dozen of his lords he rode to Nottingham. He went to the castle, where he stayed for some weeks, during which time the town was very gay. There were balls and parties and all sorts of entertainments in honour of the King.

He often used to hunt in Sherwood Forest, or even wander about there by himself. But never once did he meet Robin Hood. And Robin Hood was the very person he wanted to meet most.

Other people used still to come into Nottingham with tales of having met Robin. He still stopped all the abbots and priors and haughty knights, and made them pay toll for passing through the forest. But try how he might, King Richard never met him.

Yet Robin often saw the King, and was quite near him many times. But whenever Richard came into the forest, Robin and his men used to hide. They thought that he would probably be very angry with them for killing his deer, and for taking so much money from the haughty Norman nobles and priests. So they kept out of the way.

And because they honoured and loved the King himself, they would never have dreamed of stopping him, and of taking money away from him. Indeed Robin gave orders to his men to follow the King, if he should go to any dangerous part of the wood, so that they might protect him, and fight for him if need be. For there were many other robbers in Sherwood who were wicked men, and not just and noble like Robin.

One day the King was complaining that he had never been able to see Robin. The Bishop of Hereford heard him, and said, "If you were but a

Bishop, your Majesty, or even a plain monk, you might meet with him oftener than you cared for."

The King laughed and said nothing, but the next day he and his twelve nobles disguised themselves as monks, and rode out into the forest.

They had not gone very far before they met Robin, at the head of his men, ready to attack any rich knight or abbot who might pass that way.

As the King was very fine looking, and much taller than his nobles, Robin thought he must be an abbot at least. He was very glad to see him, as abbots always had a great deal of money, and just then Robin wanted some very much.

"He took the King's horse by the head:
Abbot, says he, abide;
I'm bound to rue such knaves as you,
That live in pomp and pride."

"But we are messengers from the King," said the King himself. "His Majesty sent us to say he would like to see you. As a sign he sends you this ring."

He held out his hand and Robin saw that he wore the King's ring.

In those days people used very seldom to write letters. When the King wished to send a message to any one he called a friend or servant, told him the message, and gave him a ring. This ring the messenger had to show as a sign that he really had come from the King. Then the person to whom the message was sent knew that he was not being deceived.

These rings were called signet rings, because a certain sign was carved upon them, which only the King might use.

Every one knew the King of England's ring. As soon as Robin saw it he knew that this must indeed be a messenger from Richard.

"God bless the King," said he, taking off his hat. "God bless all those who love him. Cursed be all those who hate him, and rebel against him."

"Then you curse yourself," said the King, "for you are a traitor."

"I am not a traitor," replied Robin, "and if you were not the King's messenger you should pay dearly for that lie.

"For I never yet hurt any man,
That honest is and true;
But those who give their minds to live
Upon other men's due.

I never hurt the husbandmen,
That use to till the ground;
Nor spill their blood that range the wood,
To follow hawk or hound.

"I fight most against monks and abbots, and take as much money as I can from them, because they steal it from poor people. They ought to live good lives, and show others a good example. But they do not. They live wicked lives, therefore they ought to be punished. If they had ruled England well, while King Richard was away, we should not have to live in the woods as we do. But come," added Robin, smiling again, "you are the King's messengers and therefore are welcome to all we have. You must come and have dinner with us now. We will make you as comfortable as we can."

The Knight and all his nobles wondered very much what kind of dinner they would get. They would much rather have gone back to Nottingham, for they thought it would be a very poor sort of dinner that Robin would be able to give them. But the King wanted to see more of Robin, so he thanked him and said they would be very pleased to come.

Robin again took hold of the King's horse and led him to the place where he and his men generally had meals.

"If you were not the King's messengers," he said with a laugh and a merry twinkle in his eye, "I fear we would not treat you quite so kindly. But as it is, if you had as much gold with you as ever I counted, I would not touch a penny of it."

Presently they arrived at a big, open space with tall trees round it. Here the King and his nobles saw that dinner was prepared for a great number of people. It looked like a large picnic, for everything was laid out on the grass.

Robin showed them where to put their horses, and where to sit. Then several page boys, dressed in green, came with large silver basins full of clean, fresh water. As the custom was in those days, they knelt on one knee, before each guest, so that he might wash his hands. The King was very much surprised to find everything so comfortable.

> "Then Robin set his horn to his mouth,
> And a loud blast did he blow,
> Till a hundred and ten of Robin Hood's men,
> Came marching all in a row.
>
> And when they came bold Robin before,
> Each man did bend his knee;
> Oh, thought the King, 'tis a gallant thing,
> And a seemly sight to see."

When the King saw that every man passed in front of Robin, and bowed to him before he went to his place, he was very much astonished. He said to himself, "These men honour their master as if he were a King. They are far more humble before him than my men are before me."

When they were all in their places, Friar Tuck said grace in Latin. Then every one sat down and dinner began.

It was a very fine dinner indeed.

> "Venison and fowls were plenty there,
> With fish out of the river;
> King Richard swore, on sea or shore,
> He never had feasted better."

Venison is the flesh of deer. No one was supposed to shoot the deer in Sherwood Forest except the King himself. When Richard saw Robin and his men feasting on his venison he hardly knew whether to be angry or to laugh.

"You say you are no traitor," said he, turning to Robin, "yet you shoot the King's deer."

"I cannot starve my men," replied Robin. "Were Richard himself here I think he would scarcely find it in his heart to grudge these fine men their food."

"Perhaps not," replied the King with a laugh; "but it is a bold thing to do. However, it is excellently cooked, and I have never enjoyed a meal better, so I at least must forgive you."

When dinner was over, Robin took a can of ale in his hand and stood up. "Let every man fill his can," said he. "Here's a health to the King."

Every man sprang to his feet, and shouting, "God save the King," drank his health.

The King himself drank to the King. He knew he must, or Robin would have found out who he was. So he stood up with the rest, and drank his own health.

"Now," said Robin, "we must amuse our guests. Get your bows and arrows and we will show what we can do in the way of archery. Shoot your very best. Shoot as if King Richard himself were here, for these gentlemen are his friends. They will tell him if you have shot well or ill when they see him again."

> "They showed such brave archery,
> By cleaving sticks and wands,
> That the King did say, such men as they,
> Live not in many lands."

"Well, Robin," then said Richard, "if I could get your pardon from the King, would you be willing to serve him and leave this wild life in the woods? Richard has need of good men and true such as you."

"Yes, with all my heart," said bold Robin Hood.

"Men, he called out, "would you be willing to serve King Richard of England—Richard Cœur de Lion?"

"Yes, with all our hearts," they shouted. Then they flung off their hoods and caps, and swore, standing bareheaded, to serve the King in everything.

"You see, Sir Abbot," said Robin, turning to him, "we are all loyal people here."

"So I see," replied the King, and his voice sounded husky.

"If you will be so kind to me as to ask the King to forgive me," went on Robin, "I think I will begin to love monks again. A Bishop was the first cause of our misfortunes, and that is what makes me hate them all. But from this day I shall try to like them again."

Then the King felt he could keep his secret no longer. He flung off the monk's hood with which he had kept his face and head covered till now, and said:—

"I am thy King, thy sovereign King,
That appears before you all;
When Robin saw that it was he,
Straight then he down did fall."

"Stand up again," said the King, "I give you your pardon gladly. Stand up, my friend, I doubt if in all England I have more faithful followers than you and your men."

When his men saw Robin kneeling they all knelt down too, wondering very much what was going to happen next. "It's the King," whispered one man who was near enough to hear what was said. "It's the King," whispered the next one. "The King, the King," whispered one after another, till every man in Robin's band knew that King Richard himself was standing before them.

When Richard had made Robin rise and stand by his side, he turned to the men and said, "I am King Richard. Are you ready to keep the oath you swore a few minutes ago? Are you ready to follow me as your master is, and be my men?"

"Stand up again," said the King.

"That we are!" they all shouted, flinging their hats in the air. "That we are! Long live King Richard! Three cheers for Richard Cœur de Lion!"

> "So they've all gone to Nottingham
> All shouting as they came,
> And when the people did them see,
> They thought the King was slain."

Such excitement there was, when it became known that Robin and his men were marching in a body to the town, shouting and singing as they came. Some people were frightened and wanted to run away, but they did not know where to run to.

Everybody wanted to see the sight. They came out of their houses and stood in the streets or leaned from the windows; all anxious to see what was happening.

"They have killed the King," some said.

"They are coming to take the town."

"They mean to hang the Sheriff."

"And all the Normans too."

"They are going to beat all the monks and friars."

"They will pull the monastery down."

The excitement grew and grew, till every one's face was red and every throat was hoarse.

"They haven't killed the King at all," some one shouted at last.

"He is riding at the head of them along with Robin Hood. Long live King Richard. Long live Robin Hood. Hurrah! Hurrah!"

> "The ploughman left his plough in the field,
>   The smith ran from his shop,
> Old folks also that scarce could go,
>   Over their sticks did hop.
>
> The King soon let them understand
>   He had been in the Green Wood;
> And from that day, for evermore,
>   Had forgiven Robin Hood."

There was great rejoicing when the people heard that Robin Hood and the King were friends. They walked up and down the streets nearly all day, singing "God Save the King."

The only person who was sorry was the Sheriff. "What! Robin Hood," said he, "that creature whom I hate?"

But Robin Hood came to him and said, "Let us be friends. I want to be friends with every one to-day. See, I have brought you back the money you paid me for your dinner in the forest."

The Sheriff was delighted to get his three hundred pounds again. He was so glad that he almost forgave Robin for all the tricks he had played.

"Now," said Robin laughingly, "I have given you back your money, so you owe me a dinner for that one I gave you in the forest. Ask the King if he will honour you by coming to supper. If he does, I will come too."

The Sheriff groaned, "If I ask the King to supper it will cost me three hundred pounds and more."

"Of course it will," replied Robin. "See that it is a fine supper, and worthy of a king."

So the poor Sheriff was obliged to ask the King to supper. He came, and so did Robin Hood. It was a very fine supper indeed. But the poor Sheriff could hardly eat anything. It made him miserable to see the King and his old enemy Robin Hood such friends. And the thought of all the money he had spent made him more miserable still. He was so unhappy that he thought he should have died.

Next day they all went off to London.

"They're all gone now to London Court,
Robin Hood and all his train;
He once was there a noble peer,
And now he's there again."

But very soon after this, unfortunately, Richard Cœur de Lion died. Prince John became King as Richard had no sons.

Prince John hated Robin, so once more he had to fly to the Green Wood with all his Merry

Men, and there he remained until he died many years after.

IX

THE DEATH OF ROBIN HOOD

Robin Hood lived to be very old. Though his hair was white, his back was straight as that of a young man. He was strong, and brave as an old lion, and his men loved and obeyed him as much as ever.

As the years went on Little John and he loved each other more and more. They were hardly ever apart.

But at last Robin began to feel weak and ill. He said sadly to Little John, "I am not able to shoot any more; my arrows will not fly. I do not know what is the matter with me. Let us go to my cousin the Prioress of Kirkley Abbey. Perhaps she will be able to cure me."

In those days there were hardly any doctors. When people were ill they used to go to clever women like the Prioress of Kirkley Abbey to be made well again.

They had a very curious way of making people well. They made a cut in the sick person's arm and let the blood flow out. After a few minutes the wound was bound up again to stop the blood flowing. This was called "bleeding."

Sometimes people got well after this. At other times they grew worse and died.

Little John and Robin set off together to Kirkley Abbey as fast as they could go. It was a difficult and painful journey. It was only a few days before Christmas. The snow lay thick on the ground, the roads were almost impassable and the cold terrible. They went bravely on, but on the journey Robin became very ill indeed—so ill that he could not sit on his horse. Along the last part of the road, Little John carried him in his arms through the deep snow.

They arrived at Kirkley Abbey on Christmas Eve. The Prioress said she was very pleased to see them. "But, good cousin Robin, what is the matter with you? You look so pale and thin."

"He is very ill," replied Little John in a broken voice. "I feared he would die on the way. I have brought him here so that you may cure him."

Then the Prioress bent over Robin and looked at him carefully. "Yes," she said, "he is very ill. I must bleed him."

If Little John had seen the face of the Prioress, as she bent over his master, he would have taken him away again. There was such a wicked look upon it. But he did not see.

"Come, good Little John," she said, turning to him, "I have a pleasant room on the south side of the abbey looking towards your dear Sherwood. Take up my cousin and carry him there."

So Little John took Robin in his arms and followed the Prioress down the cool, quiet passages, to the little room on the south side of the abbey.

It was very still and peaceful in this little room, which was far away from where the other people in the abbey lived.

Little John wanted to stay beside Robin, but the Prioress said, "No, he must have perfect quietness if he is to get better."

"I will not move nor make a sound," said Little John, "if you will only let me stay."

"No," said the Prioress again, "I must be alone with him if I am to make him better."

"When may I come back, then?" asked Little John.

"In a few hours, perhaps. Perhaps tomorrow morning," replied the Prioress. "I will call you when it is time."

So with a very heavy heart Little John walked away. He went out into the abbey garden. There he sat down under a tree where he could watch the window of Robin's room. Hour after hour he waited patiently in the cold.

Now the Prioress was a bad woman. Robin had always been very kind to her, and she had pretended to love him. Really she hated him, and longed to hurt him.

As long as Robin was well and strong she could do nothing that would hurt him. But now that he had come to her, weak and ill, he was in her power. She meant not to cure him, but to kill him. That was why she sent Little John away. She was a very wicked woman indeed.

As soon as she was alone with him the Prioress made a cut in Robin's arm so that the blood flowed out. She pretended to bind the wound up again, but she put the bandage on so badly that the blood flowed all the same. Then she locked Robin in the room and went away.

Robin was so weak and weary that he soon fell asleep. He slept for many hours. And all the time Little John sat patiently under the tree in the garden—waiting.

When Robin woke he found he was so weak that he could hardly move. He saw the blood was still flowing from his arm and knew that if it was not stopped he would soon die.

He tried to raise himself to the window, but he had not strength. Then he thought of his bugle-horn. With great difficulty he put it to his mouth, and blew three faint blasts.

> "Then said Little John on hearing him,
> As he sat under the tree,
> I fear my master is near dead,
> He blows so wearily."

Little John sprang up, and ran as fast as he could to the room in which Robin was lying. The door was locked, so he put his shoulder against it and burst it open. There he found his master almost dead.

Carefully and quickly he bound up the arm. His heart was full of love and grief for his master, and of anger against the wicked Prioress.

"Grant me one favour, master," he said.

"What favour is it you would ask, dear Little John?" replied Robin.

"It is that you will give me leave to gather all our men together, and bring them here to burn this abbey, and kill the wicked Prioress as she has killed you."

"Now nay, now nay, quoth Robin Hood,
That boon I'll not grant thee,
I never hurt a woman in all my life.
Nor man in woman's company:
I never hurt fair maid in all my life,
Nor at my end shall it be."

So Little John promised he would not try to punish the wicked Prioress. But his heart was full of anger against her.

Robin lay still for a short time, and Little John knelt beside him. Then he said, "Little John, I should like to shoot once more. Carry me to the window. Give me my good bow into my hands, and hold me up while I shoot. Where the arrow falls there bury me."

So Little John lifted him up and held him while he shot. The arrow only went a very little way and fell in the garden, not far from where Little John had been sitting.

"It was a good shot, master, a very good shot," said Little John, though he could hardly speak for tears.

"Was it indeed, friend? I could not see," replied Robin, "but you will bury me where it fell."

"Lay me a green sod under my head,
And another at my feet,
And lay my bent bow by my side,
Which was my music sweet;
And make my grave of gravel and green,
Which is most right and meet.

Let me have length and breadth enough,
With a green sod at my head,
That they may say when I am dead,
Here lies bold Robin Hood."

Little John promised to do everything as Robin asked.

"Thank you, dear friend, good-bye," whispered Robin, and he lay still in Little John's arms.

"Thank you, dear friend, good-bye."

Presently he raised himself up, and looking eagerly out of the window, "Was it indeed a good shot?" he said.

Then he fell back again—dead.

Just at that moment the convent bells began to ring for the Christmas Eve service. Through the open window came the sound of the sweet voices of the nuns singing a Christmas carol.

> "It is the vigil holy,
> The Eve of Noël fair,
> When Christ the King comes lowly
> Man's miseries to share.
>
> Our sins are clean forgiven,
> Our injuries forgot,
> And Kneeling pure and shriven,
> We wait the birth of God."

But Robin was dead. Never again would he hear the sweet Christmas carol he had loved so well.

Beside him knelt Little John almost broken-hearted.

There was great sorrow all through the land, when it became known that Robin Hood was dead. There was also great anger against the Prioress, but no one tried to punish her, because Robin had asked them to spare her.

Little John called all the Merry Men together for the last time, and they buried their master where his last arrow fell, in the garden of Kirkley Abbey, in Yorkshire.

Over the grave they placed a stone, and carved upon it these lines:—

> "Here, underneath this stone,
>   Lies Robert, Earl of Huntingdon;
> No archer ever was so good,
>   The people called him Robin Hood.
> Such outlaws as he and his men
>   Will England never see again."

CPSIA information can be obtained
at www.ICGtesting.com
Printed in the USA
BVHW08s1441070618
518478BV00001B/78/P

9 781599 150017